The Accidental Parent

Nurturing Love in Unforeseen Circumstances

Adrienne Alexander-Allen

ISBN: 979-8-9884620-1-9

DEDICATION

This book is dedicated to Willie Lee Alexander, my mother, who stepped in and stood in the gap when my biological mother couldn't.

This book is also dedicated to you, the ***Accidental Parent*** who, despite unforeseen circumstances, strives to be the best example and support system for your children. Your resilience, compassion, and dedication are truly inspiring, and this book is a tribute to your journey.

Contents

ACKNOWLEDGMENTS

Writing The Accidental Parent: Nurturing Love in Unforeseen Circumstances has been a journey filled with reflection, growth, and deep gratitude. This book would not have been possible without the support and encouragement of the many special people who keep me pushing through even when I feel like giving up.

First and foremost, I want to express my heartfelt thanks to my beloved family. To my husband, Floyd, your love and patience have been a constant source of strength and consistency. To my four wonderful children, Duane, Aleeah, Joshua, and Justin, who have each taught me invaluable lessons about love, resilience, and the beauty of life's unexpected twists. And to my babies, my three adorable grandchildren, Iaia, Ava, and DJ, who brighten my day without trying.

A special thank you to my partner in crime, my food best friend, Charlene; your friendship has been the rock I know I can always lean on and has been used constantly during the highs and lows of this journey. Your understanding, humor, and kindness have been a guiding light, and our conversations have provided me with so much clarity and inspiration,

To DeBlair, a cherished friend who began as a client and evolved into a genuine confidante. Your insight and support have been instrumental in shaping this book, and I'm grateful for your unwavering belief in me.

I'm also grateful to my readers. Thank you for taking the time to engage with my story. I hope ***The Accidental Parent*** resonates with you and offers insight and comfort in your journey.

Lastly, to everyone who has been a part of my life's path, thank you for your presence and impact. This book is a testament to the love and connection that emerge from unforeseen circumstances.

With deepest gratitude,

Adrienne

Preface

To summarize this season of my life, I'm a 50-year-old woman who was entirely unprepared for the 4-year-old in my care. Four years ago, when I celebrated my youngest child's high school graduation, the occasion meant more to me than seeing him cross the stage for a piece of paper. It meant I was finally free of the struggle to get him up in the morning to be on time for school. This meant there would be no more parent-teacher conferences to discuss behavior and academic performance. And it meant I would no longer waste my breath on motherly lectures that seemed to go in one ear and out the other. I was elated, but the celebration was short-lived as I soon became my granddaughter's caregiver. Don't be mistaken; I love her with every fiber of my being and would go to war for her. However, I would not have believed it if I had been told four years ago that I would be starting the motherhood journey again from scratch. Yet, there I was—an accidental parent.

The similarities between caring for my granddaughter and my early life are surreal. Due to my parents' struggle with alcoholism and drug addiction, I was also raised by my grandparents. It serves as a generational reference point when grandparents become *new* parents by accident, and they usually do so without as much of a discussion to determine if raising a child who isn't theirs aligns with their goals. The phrase "do what you gotta do" rings true for many of them.

Looking back over my formative years, I realize how much I didn't experience being raised by grandparents well into their sixties.

I can't overlook how truly blessed I was, but while all my *needs* were met, my *wants* were lacking—wanting love, wanting company, wanting siblings. There weren't many activities with senior parents other than watching the "stories," learning to cook and attending church services five days a week. So, that was my childhood in a nutshell.

Their structured, mature lifestyle caused me to grow up quickly. I landed my first job as a Blue Chip-In tutor in middle school to attain some of my *wants*, which was my priority. Because there was an entire generation between us, it was hard for my accidental parents to see my *wants* as necessary. My upbringing motivates me to provide a different experience for my granddaughter.

While I'm younger than my grandparents were when they stepped in to care for me, age is not what makes the difference. I'm determined to love my granddaughter out loud, ensuring she understands that her present circumstances are not her fault. Love, compassion, and understanding are a recipe for a good life, and I am committed to sharing it with her above everything else.

My granddaughter is the most loving, kind, generous, thoughtful, and adorable four-year-old walking the earth. (And it doesn't hurt that she's an Aquarius like her grandmother, with a birthday just nine days before mine.) She's perfect for me and captures the heart of anyone she meets. I wouldn't trade her for the world. However, as an accidental parent, I was struggling.

I can't say I was mentally or financially prepared or possessed the strength and ability to take on this role, but I did. And if some believe that I had a choice in the matter by opting to take my granddaughter in rather than allow her to be placed in foster care or passed along to other relatives, I did not. She's family, and belongs with me, so no other option exists in my mind. Despite the challenges, being separated from my granddaughter is never an option. I intend to power through adversity and overcome the hardships of being an *accidental parent.*

Introduction

How Did I Get Here?

It was 3 a.m. when a detective called. He was looking for my daughter. She was home and had been for a while since picking up my son from work earlier that evening. I had no idea what the call was about, but it gradually became apparent that whatever it was was serious. My world started to crumble around me when I got the call. Reality became a blur because this couldn't be my life; I wasn't one to get phone calls from the police in the middle of the night.

The truth of it is my daughter is like many strong-willed young adults. She would do the opposite if something I said seemed the right decision. We bumped heads regularly, and any conversation about what was at the root of our conflict was nonexistent. When I found out about her pregnancy, we discussed her course of action, how she felt, and the child's father, whom I still haven't met to this day. In all these years, our interaction has been limited to social media.

At the time, my daughter was adamant that she was ready to be a mom and insisted that discussing it was unnecessary. This decision frustrated me because my daughter lived in my home, couldn't keep a job, and just wasn't ready—in my opinion—to have a child.

My feelings would be further confirmed when she was in her second trimester, and the nightmare began. Little did I know my granddaughter's father was involved in some questionable activities. My daughter was in love, and her judgment was clouded by what she felt for him.

After nearly a year of talking to public defenders and traveling to court dates, I was still unaware of the whole story. I wouldn't learn the gravity of the situation until my daughter received five years in prison, which initiated my journey as an *accidental parent.*

And to be clear, accidental parenthood is a situation where individuals become parents unexpectedly or under unconventional circumstances due to the absence or incapacity of biological parents. Whether it be guardianship or kinship care, foster care, adoption, or informal caregiving arrangements, accidental parenting comes with a unique set of challenges that tend to impact a caregiver financially, physically, mentally, and emotionally.

As I weather the occasional storms of becoming an accidental parent, I wanted to extend a guiding hand, a comforting presence, and an inspiring voice to individuals who find themselves unexpectedly thrust into the role of parenting. Unforeseen circumstances, sudden changes in life circumstances, or the absence of biological parents could leave many grasping for strength and encouragement. I aim to offer a beacon of light amidst uncertainty.

At its core, *The Accidental Parent* is a testament to the resilience, strength, and love that defines the journey of accidental parenthood. It serves as a companion for those navigating uncharted territory. It provides a roadmap filled with practical advice, emotional support, and empowering insights to navigate accidental parenthood's legal, emotional, and real-world complexities. From understanding legal rights and responsibilities to managing the day-to-day challenges of parenting, this book will help you gain confidence and clarity.

This is more than just a guidebook; it offers a supportive embrace to those who may feel isolated or overwhelmed by their circumstances. It is also a journal to share with my daughter, my granddaughter, and future generations about the power of family, whether biological or accidental.

Above all, this book celebrates the strength, resilience, and love that defines accidental parenthood. Through this journey of courage, perseverance, and transformation, I hope you're inspired to embrace your roles as accidental parents with newfound confidence, strength, and hope. Understand that despite the challenges you may face, you have the power to create a bright and fulfilling future for yourself and your families.

Allow this work to be a constant offering of encouragement, support, and validation to those who have faced or are facing unexpected challenges. However, it is imperative that you also tune into moments of profound joy, growth, and connection because they will present themselves among the chaos.

There is power in the human spirit, and love can help transcend even the most unexpected circumstances. I hope you will find solace in knowing you are not alone.

CHAPTER ONE

Facing Reality

My granddaughter has been in my care since 2021, and starting life over as the parent of a toddler was utterly unexpected. One moment, I was making plans for my future, and without warning, I was thrust back into full-time parenthood. The instant shift in lifestyle was earth-shattering, and I couldn't imagine how I would ever adjust, but I remained hopeful.

Acceptance of my new reality didn't come easy. Initially, I tried to brush off any resistance because caring for my granddaughter was my decision, and my only option was to accept it. However, realizing that I was becoming an accidental parent was a phase marked by shock, denial, and an overwhelming sense of loss. I was again preparing to lose myself to carry the weight and responsibility of having a small child. The children I birthed were grown, and I could finally travel, move freely, and focus on my marriage, but that reality would quickly fade. The sudden shift in my life's trajectory created an internal battle that I was losing.

The initial shock of becoming a full-time caregiver again was paralyzing. I was extremely overwhelmed by the weight of my new responsibilities. Raising a toddler after 20 years of watching my own children mature from infancy to adulthood was a hard pill to swallow. In the face of such profound upheaval, happiness was hard to maintain as I clung to the hope that things would somehow return to normal. I faced my circumstances head-on and did everything I could, but I was caught in a whirlwind of emotions that ranged from disbelief to anger and sadness. I was mourning the life I once knew and my dreams and plans for the future.

Grief was a constant companion in this phase and was manifested through intense waves of sadness and longing. I missed my independence and grappled with feelings of guilt and regret. I even wondered if I could have done something differently to avoid my circumstances altogether. However, despite the pain and turmoil, there was a glimmer of hope, but it did not come in the form of immediate peace and answers to each of my challenges.

To start, I had to acknowledge the reality of my circumstances while recognizing my resilience to overcome adversity. I discovered that it was about embracing the journey of healing and allowing myself to grieve what was lost while also finding strength in the opportunity for growth and renewal. Amid the upheaval and momentary lapse of direction, there was an opportunity to find meaning in the chaos. I now had the chance to reassess my priorities, redefine my sense of self, and discover new sources of purpose and fulfillment. I've come to understand that while the road ahead may be uncertain, there is power in embracing the unknown and trusting in my ability to navigate whatever challenges come my way.

Here are some tips I've gathered that helped me to face reality and overcome the hardships of accidental parenting, and they can help you, too:

Acknowledge and validate your feelings. Allow yourself to acknowledge and accept the range of emotions you may be experiencing, whether it's grief, anger, guilt, or sadness. Remember that it's normal to feel overwhelmed by the challenges of accidental parenthood, and your feelings are valid.

Seek support. Don't hesitate to ask for help from friends, family members, or support groups who understand what you're going through. Talking to others who have shared similar experiences can provide validation, empathy, and practical advice for coping with emotional challenges.

Practice self-compassion. Be kind to yourself and practice self-compassion during difficult times. Recognize that you're doing your best under challenging circumstances and give yourself credit for your efforts and accomplishments, no matter how small they may seem.

Take breaks and practice self-care. Make time for self-care activities that help you relax, recharge, and rejuvenate. Whether it's taking a walk, practicing mindfulness or meditation, engaging in a hobby, or simply taking a few moments to yourself, prioritizing self-care can help reduce stress and improve your overall well-being.

Set realistic expectations. Be realistic about what you can reasonably accomplish as an accidental parent, and avoid putting too much pressure on yourself to be perfect. Remember that it's okay to ask for help when you need it, and it's essential to prioritize your own well-being along with your child's needs.

Focus on the positive. While it's natural to dwell on the challenges and difficulties of accidental parenthood, try to focus on the positive aspects of your situation as well. Celebrate the moments of joy, connection, and growth you experience with your child, and cultivate gratitude for the blessings in your life, however small they may seem.

Seek professional help if needed. If you're struggling to cope with the emotional impact of accidental parenthood, don't hesitate to seek professional help from a therapist or counselor who specializes in working with parents and caregivers. Professional support can provide you with additional tools, strategies, and insights for managing your emotions and improving your overall well-being.

Ultimately, facing the reality of accidental parenting is about finding the resilience to confront life's unexpected twists and turns. It's about embracing the truth of our circumstances, no matter how difficult, and finding the courage to move forward with grace and determination. In the face of adversity, we discover our strength and capacity for growth. And through this process of facing reality, we begin to write the next chapter of our story.

CHAPTER TWO

Navigating the New World

I can't fully emphasize the importance of having support in this season. Personally, it took a while for me to open myself up enough to ask for the help I needed. It was like being in a bubble that no one could pop. Although I knew the value of community, for some crazy reason, I thought I could do it alone.

For those like me, asking for help can be incredibly difficult. Feelings of shame or inadequacy prevent us from reaching out to others for support. We must break down these barriers and embrace vulnerability as a strength rather than a weakness.

Accidental parenthood can easily break someone unprepared, which is what most of us are. We are immediately bombarded with the need to research laws related to guardianship, custody, adoption, and parental rights. As accidental parents, we must educate ourselves on the benefits available to us and establish legal authority to protect ourselves and the child's rights. As we begin this process, you're flooded with legal documentation, court proceedings, and numerous other formal requirements, which take time and money.

While duties required to care for a child legally weren't in the plans of an accidental parent, they are unavoidable. In addition to the legal stressors, accidental parents may encounter financial strain, housing instability, and limited access to healthcare and education, all while balancing caregiving responsibilities with other obligations.; not to mention the frustration that may arise when the presence of a significant other, or other adults in the home, does not yield support. We must understand that our decision to care for a child does not automatically obligate those connected to us. Otherwise, we may find that our relationships are tested. And while the tasks seem endless and impossible for one person to carry, know that you are not alone.

One of the first steps in building a support system is reaching out to others who can empathize and understand. Whether it's friends, family members, or fellow support group members, connecting with those who have walked a similar path can provide a sense of validation and solidarity.

I was surprised by the outpouring of support from friends and family when they discovered my new guardian role, but I questioned if it was genuine in the back of my mind. *Do they really want to help, or do they just want to be in my business?* This question played a considerable part in keeping me silent, telling as few people as possible what was happening.

Stay Grounded

Feeling like I had to do everything alone was overwhelming, so I created the ***JOY BALM***. This practice creates serenity amidst the chaos and challenges of accidental parenthood and invokes strength, grace, and joy.

JOY: Juggle (responsibilities), Open (to help), Yield (to imperfection). When you're feeling overwhelmed, remember JOY. Instead of drowning in stress, *juggle* your responsibilities with grace, *open* up to accept help from others, and *yield* to imperfection, knowing that it's okay not to have it all together. Embrace JOY and find peace within the chaos of parenting.

BALM: Breaks, Assistance, Love, Mindfulness. In the whirlwind of parenthood, find your BALM. Take *breaks* to recharge when needed, seek *assistance* from your support system, infuse everything with *love*, and practice *mindfulness* to stay present and grounded. BALM can soothe your soul and restore balance to your parenting journey.

Know that you are a valuable and essential part of a child's life, and your resilience and strength should be celebrated and acknowledged, but it must first begin with you. Celebrate even the most minor victories and pat yourself on the back.

Find the Proper Resources

Mental and emotional challenges aside, even with self-motivation, the physical and financial hardships of accidental parenting also need exploration. Many communities offer financial assistance programs for families facing economic hardship, including accidental parents. These programs may provide financial aid for basic needs such as housing, food, utilities, and childcare expenses.

Government assistance programs such as Temporary Assistance for Needy Families (TANF), Supplemental Nutrition Assistance Program (SNAP), and housing assistance programs can support accidental parents struggling to make ends meet.

Be sure to research local nonprofit organizations and charities offering financial assistance programs designed to support families in crises; these organizations can provide access to essential resources and support networks, including food banks, clothing closets, homeless shelters, and counseling services. Community Centers and family resource centers often offer a range of programs and services tailored to the needs of families, including parenting classes, support groups, and childcare assistance. In addition, public libraries, schools, and churches may also offer community programs and services to support families, such as free educational workshops, recreational activities, and volunteer opportunities.

Beyond meeting household needs, support networks are crucial in providing emotional support, practical assistance, and social connections. If time does not permit in-person meet-ups, online support groups, and forums can provide a valuable source of support and camaraderie for accidental parents. They allow us to connect with others facing similar challenges and share advice, tips, and resources.

By discovering financial assistance programs, community services, and support networks, accidental parents can access the resources they need to minimize the challenges of parenthood. However, we must never forget that it is okay to ask for help, especially regarding our emotional health, which is essential to being a resilient and effective parent.

You are not alone in your journey. Know that you possess the resilience, strength, and capacity to overcome challenges, even if it requires some help. So, take advantage of the many resources and support networks available to help you navigate the journey, implement self-care practices, increase self-compassion, and set realistic expectations to move forward confidently.

CHAPTER THREE

Parenting Through Adversity

Stereotypes and misconceptions surrounding accidental parenthood can often lead to misunderstanding and stigma. You may ask, "What beliefs or misconceptions exist, and where do they come from?" The answer depends upon the reason a person became an accidental parent.

For instance, a traumatic experience, like the death or incapacity of a biological parent, may present adversity that requires you to navigate a complex array of emotions within yourself and the child. The emotional rollercoaster accompanying the parenting journey can be challenging, and it is vital to acknowledge and process these emotions effectively.

Misconceptions about how or why a child was placed in your care can create an additional layer of stress and frustration if you are assumed to be unfit. Additionally, the belief that accidental parenthood results from personal failure can also show up in your experience, but it isn't always true. Family crises such as substance abuse, domestic violence, or financial instability can also lead to accidental parenthood, and relatives or close friends may step in to provide care and stability for the children involved. Not to mention that acts of selflessness, such as taking in a child in need or becoming a foster parent, can also result in accidental parenthood.

I've said it before, and I'll repeat it: overcoming feelings of self-doubt and inadequacy is one of the most significant challenges of parenting through adversity. Whether it's questioning your ability to meet the needs of a child or grappling with feelings of guilt and shame, building self-confidence and leaning on others in the face of doubt will help win the battle.

By fully supporting the primary caregiver in the accidental parenting dilemma, we also support the child who has temporarily lost or will never again have, access to their biological parent. The responsibility is not an easy undertaking and requires a well-informed village mature enough to rise to the occasion without distracting from the goal.

To help guide you through challenging conversations, here are a few general tips for those connected to, or those who support, accidental parents:

Be empathetic and avoid making assumptions. Recognize that accidental parenthood can arise from various circumstances, many of which may be beyond an individual's control. Avoid making assumptions about why someone became an accidental parent and instead approach the situation with empathy and understanding.

Offer support without judgment. If you know someone who is an accidental parent, offer your support without passing judgment on their situation. Whether it's providing a listening ear, offering practical assistance, or simply being there for emotional support, your kindness can make a world of difference.

Educate yourself and others. Take the time to educate yourself and others about the realities of accidental parenthood. Challenge misconceptions and stereotypes by sharing information about the diverse circumstances that can lead to accidental parenthood and the resilience of accidental parents.

Advocate for systemic support. Recognize the need for systemic support for accidental parents and their families. Advocate for policies and programs that provide resources and assistance to help accidental parents navigate their roles and responsibilities more effectively.

Offer practical help. If you can, offer practical help to accidental parents facing challenges, including providing childcare, helping with household tasks, or offering financial assistance to ease their burden.

Show compassion and understanding. Above all, show compassion and understanding towards accidental parents. Recognize the strength it takes to navigate the challenges of accidental parenthood and offer your support however possible.

In conclusion, we must confront stereotypes and misconceptions to shed light on the reality of accidental or unintentional parenthood. Doing so empowers the individual and provides support for their newfound endeavor.

CHAPTER FOUR

Requesting and Providing Help

The burden of unexpectedly raising a child can be pretty lonely, and those around you may want to help but are unsure of how to approach the situation. As mentioned in the previous chapter, supporting an accidental parent requires sensitivity and understanding; otherwise, your help may not be helpful. However, there are tips and techniques to help move the relationship forward if you or someone close to you has become an accidental parent.

First, when sharing your truth, you must welcome and understand assertive communication from both sides. Assertive communication allows everyone to express their thoughts, feelings and needs in a transparent, respectful, and confident manner while also respecting the rights and boundaries of others. It allows accidental parents to assert themselves effectively in their personal relationships and interactions with professionals and institutions.

Second, make sure to clearly state your needs, boundaries, and expectations during personal and professional interactions. Also, if needed, set boundaries around invasive questions or intrusive advice while advocating for yourself. People sometimes feel entitled to know the who, what, when, and why, but remember, you're not obligated to answer or respond to questions you think violate your space.

Third, pay attention to your body language when feeling offended or turned off. Body language plays a crucial role in assertive communication. Ensure you maintain eye contact, use open and confident body language, and speak in a clear and assertive tone to effectively convey your message.

One way to do this is to use “I” statements to express your feelings, thoughts, and concerns assertively. Adding an “I” statement is a great way to focus on your own feelings and experiences to minimize your focus on what the other person has done or has failed to do.

Being certified in conflict resolution and conflict management, “I” statements have become my favorite resolution tool. It’s the difference between saying, “You’re always judging me,” and “I feel judged when you make comments about my parenting.” Communicating your feelings in this way encourages understanding as you share your truth and avoid placing blame.

Fourth, to communicate assertively, be sure to practice active listening. Fully engage with and understand the other person’s perspective before responding. Be sure to actively listen to their concerns before jumping to conclusions or interrupting to advocate for your needs.

Fifth, as a support system, encourage accidental parents to embrace assertive self-advocacy to challenge stereotypes and promote understanding. By assertively communicating their experiences, needs, and preferences, accidental parents can challenge misconceptions, assert their rights, and promote greater understanding and acceptance within their personal relationships and interactions with professionals and institutions.

Assertive self-advocacy empowers accidental parents to take control of their narratives, assert their identities, and demand respect and recognition for their unique experiences and challenges. It allows us to challenge stereotypes, dispel misconceptions, and foster greater community empathy and understanding.

Building self-confidence and self-esteem while focusing on strengths and accomplishments as a parent is possible. Therefore, as you navigate the complexities of accidental parenting through adversity, remember to acknowledge and celebrate your strength. You have already overcome immense challenges, so use your past victories as a blueprint to fully trust in your ability to overcome whatever obstacles come your way. You possess the inner strength to persevere.

One of the most powerful tools in this situation is the bond you share with your child. Nurture and cherish this connection, drawing strength and inspiration from your love. Take time to engage in meaningful activities together, create memories, and build a foundation of trust and understanding that will sustain you both through difficult times.

And remember, you do not have to navigate this journey alone. Reach out to friends, family members, support groups, or mental health professionals who can offer guidance, encouragement, and practical assistance. Surround yourself with a network of support that uplifts and empowers you, providing a safe space to express your emotions and receive help when needed.

Finally, remember to prioritize self-care and well-being while caring for your child. Take time to rest, recharge, and engage in activities that bring you joy and fulfillment. Set boundaries around your time and energy, and understand that taking care of yourself is essential to caring for others effectively.

Though the path may be challenging, beauty and meaning can be found along the journey of accidental parenting. Embrace the lessons and insights that come from facing difficult circumstances and recognize the growth and transformation that occur along the way.

Ultimately, remember that accidental parenting is not just about surviving – it's about thriving. It's about embracing the fullness of life's experiences, finding strength in vulnerability, and discovering your resilience to overcome obstacles. You are stronger than you know, and your journey is a testament to the love, courage, and perseverance it takes to weather the storms of parenthood.

CHAPTER FIVE

Adjusting to Life as An Accidental Parent

Adjusting to unexpected parenthood often involves significant changes, including priorities, routines, relationships, and self-identity shifts. Being raised by my grandmother, I didn't recognize how big of an undertaking it was to care for a grandchild. However, I now understand that embracing change is crucial to navigating accidental parenthood.

As I reflect on how my presence as a child created a noticeable shift in my grandparents' priorities, I cannot help but wonder if they resented being hindered from enjoying retirement age. My grandmother was a stay-at-home wife when I came to live with them, but that didn't negate any need she may have had for silence or personal time and space, which are hard to come by with a child in the midst.

Because my placement in their home was a non-traditional arrangement, my grandparents' process of completing paperwork or any legal dealings was less tedious. There was no official custody agreement. I was just there, and they were my accidental parents.

My early years were spent attending school, watching soap operas, visiting family, and taking the occasional crabbing trip with my great-grandmother. I was blessed with the stability of a grandmother who cooked three meals a day, ironed clothes fresh from the clothesline, ensured I was in school on time, and took my seat in church each Sunday. These routines have been monumental in creating the person I am today and preparing me to become an accidental parent myself.

I never wondered how or why I came to live with my grandparents until I became older and noticed the family dynamics of friends and neighbors. *Was I missing out on something?* Absolutely! My grandparents and I did very little together—if anything at all—while other families would hang out at the mall, go on family vacations, or frequent restaurants and movie theaters. I had a roof over my head, clothes on my back, and food on the table, and that was enough for them.

Being raised as an only child by grandparents can be lonely—at least in my household, it was. There was minimal affection, no birthday parties, and any talk about the birds and the bees was nonexistent. It was simply me, my imagination, and my books.

This loneliness forced me to become self-reliant at a young age. I learned to entertain myself, finding solace in the pages of books and the worlds they created. Reading became my escape, a way to experience adventures and emotions that were absent in my own life. I developed a rich inner world and a vivid imagination, which became my constant companions.

There were times when the emotional void felt overwhelming. I craved the kind of nurturing and guidance that seemed so abundant in other families. The absence of open affection and communication left me to navigate many of life's questions and challenges alone. My grandparents provided the basics, but emotional support was something I had to find elsewhere and something my granddaughter will never have to search for as long as I'm around.

As I grew older, I began to see the strength that came from my independence. The skills I developed out of necessity became assets. I was resourceful, resilient, and capable of handling situations many of my peers found daunting. My self-reliance, born out of loneliness, became a cornerstone of my identity. I was always the life of the party and the center of attention because it's what I had longed for since adolescence.

And as I matured, I better understood my grandparents' sacrifices. They were of a generation with differing values and ways of expressing themselves and how much they care. They prioritized ensuring I had the essentials—food, shelter, and education. While they may not have shown affection in the ways I'd yearned for, their dedication and hard work were their expression of love. My newfound understanding helped me appreciate their efforts more deeply and recognize how they silently supported me.

Despite the emotional distance, my grandparents instilled many important values. They taught me the importance of hard work, responsibility, and perseverance. My grandfather, who was a man of few words, demonstrated his love through his actions, which ultimately yielded my ability to grow a cucumber vine, ensure the bills were paid, and maintain a stable home environment.

Though not overly affectionate, my grandmother showed her care by preparing meals and managing the household with unwavering dedication. To this day, I tell people my grandmother was the epitome of womanhood, the picture-perfect form of a housewife in real life.

Though rare, moments of connection stood out amidst the routine. I remember when my grandmother would share stories of her youth, offering glimpses into her world and struggles. Though often told in passing, these stories became cherished memories that helped me understand her better and feel closer to her.

Adolescence brought its own set of challenges. Without traditional parental guidance, I had to figure out many things on my own, including how to navigate friendships, understand my identity, and manage teenage pressures and struggles. The lack of open communication with my grandparents meant I turned to friends, teachers, and sometimes even books for advice and support. It also included the occasional bad decision, hanging with the wrong company, and making mistakes.

Teachers and mentors at school played crucial roles in my life. They provided the encouragement and guidance that I sometimes missed at home. Extracurricular activities became my outlet to connect with others and explore my interests. These experiences helped fill some gaps and provided a sense of belonging that I craved.

My stepmother, Celeste Thomas, also played a role in my growth. Her advice and guidance helped me to make decisions that greatly impacted my future.

Looking back, I can see how these experiences shaped me into who I am today. Recognizing what I missed and my feelings about the lack of affection in my childhood makes me want to love those around me out loud so they never have to question my love for them. The loneliness and independence also birthed the self-sufficiency that has served me well. While I may have missed out on specific familial experiences, I gained a unique perspective on life and learned to find strength within myself.

Now that I find myself in my grandparents' shoes, unexpectedly raising a granddaughter, I advise others in similar situations to seek out and build their own support networks. Whether through community organizations or hobbies, finding places where you feel understood and valued can make a significant difference.

Healing and moving on from a childhood marked by unexpected parenthood is a journey of understanding and acceptance. If you're like me, you will recognize the sacrifices of those who raised you, find strength in the challenges you faced, and use your experiences for growth and transformation. My story is just one of many, and I hope it resonates with those who have walked a similar path. By sharing our stories, we can find common ground, support one another, and move forward with hope and strength.

CHAPTER SIX

Reflections on Accidental Parenthood

Accidental parenthood, with all its challenges, can also lead to profound growth and connection, revealing the human heart's extraordinary capacity to adapt and thrive. To better understand the diverse experiences of accidental parenthood, I reached out to individuals who had either taken on accidental parenting or were raised by someone who had. Their responses to my questionnaire provide a rich tapestry of perspectives and highlight common themes. Their voices reflect the diversity and complexity of accidental parenthood.

These stories of resilience, love, and perseverance provide a window into the lives of those who navigate this unexpected journey. Allow their collective wisdom and personal experiences to offer a deeper understanding of the challenges, triumphs, and transformative moments that define accidental parenthood. By sharing these experiences, we hope to provide solace, guidance, and inspiration to others walking a similar path. As an FYI, all of the names have been changed to protect the respondent's identities.

John's Story

Describe the circumstances that led you to be raised by someone other than your parents.

My grandparents raised me due to my mother's addiction to crack cocaine and her being a prostitute. As a result of negligence due to her drug habit and a lack of responsible parenting, my mother lost all four of her children. My grandparents took legal custody of me and my sister, while my late aunt and uncle cared for my two oldest brothers.

How did you first learn about your unique family dynamics, and what were your initial thoughts and feelings?

I learned of my unique circumstances as early as elementary school. Growing up, it was customary to be at my grandparents' house and have them take me to school, bring me home, and spend lots of time with them. It wasn't until elementary school that I actually unearthed the whole story and discovered that my mother had been on drugs, and as a result, we were being raised by them.

What were some challenges you faced?

I've never been close to my mother, so my connection with her feels more like a distant aunt or cousin relationship. And it is also unfortunate that I didn't have a relationship with my brothers, even though they lived only five minutes away. Another challenge I faced was seeing my mother help raise the children of women she dated while neglecting her own children.

How did your relationship with your new family shape your childhood and adolescence?

My grandparents helped to shape my life positively. Even though they were older, they kept me grounded and stable, which enabled me to excel academically. However, seeing my mom high and nearly overdosed when I was so young demonstrated how much there was to understand outside the innocent veil of childhood. Through my grandparents, I could grasp the purpose of hard work, make responsible decisions, and understand the effects of trauma and how it can damage a person's life. My grandmother was a counselor, so she made sure that my sister and I understood the reality of being raised by them. She emphasized the importance of not internalizing our situation so it didn't have lasting effects.

In what ways do you feel your upbringing was different from your peers?

My upbringing was very different. I've seen more drugs sold and ingested than the average person has ever experienced. I grew up fast because of my mother's addiction. It was a lifestyle that included going to drug houses to find my mom and seeing her nearly die from a drug overdose.

The environment greatly impacted my experience at school. I attended a Montessori school with many affluent students who couldn't identify or understand my family dynamics. With wealthy parents who were very active in their lives and at school, they could not understand why my grandparents raised me. It was different, and I knew that early on, so I didn't share much about my mom and home life during my formative years. Most of my friends, teachers, and coaches knew of my grandparents but little about my mom. It is the same to this day.

What positive aspects or strengths did you gain from being raised in this situation?

I gained keen insight into the importance of having my own and being independent. I was also exceptional in school, which ensured I had an opportunity to excel and not have the same experience as my mom. A positive aspect is that it helped me gain wisdom from older people who had already experienced at least six decades of life. The knowledge I acquired from them as a youngster greatly exceeded others my age. And to this day, people assume I'm older than I am.

What advice would you give someone who has found themselves in this situation?

First, I would tell them to go to therapy and not internalize it. While our parents may write our story's introduction or first chapter, we must remember that they do not pen the entire book. Second, since being raised by grandparents can be challenging because of so many emotions, they must be easy on themselves. Sometimes, you may feel appreciative yet still long for your birth parents, and there is nothing wrong with that. Third, holidays and parent days (Mother's Day and Father's Day) can also be difficult, especially when it's trending on social media, so try to take a break. And fourth, I would also say that when the time is right internally, have a conversation with your birth parent to free yourself from the hurt and disappointment you experienced as a result of their actions.

What support systems or resources were most helpful to you in your experience?

My cousin was an immense support. Also, being part of my fraternity's youth auxiliary group helped mold and develop me. I've received guidance from many positive male examples who were able to help and assist my grandfather.

What strategies did you find effective in managing this situation's emotional and practical challenges?

Therapy and writing helped me the most. I wrote two books (unpublished) about the dynamics of being raised by my grandmother and my attempt to build a relationship with the mom who didn't raise me.

What is the most important thing for parents to remember as they navigate this unexpected journey?

Some of the best advice I can give any parent is to allow the child to form their own opinion of their absent parent—the good and the bad—and not to downplay the parent. If the parent is absent and doesn't want to be around, let them have that ah-ha moment in their own time and come to that understanding. Sometimes, through anger and frustration resulting from the parent's absence, grandparents can let their thoughts and emotions seep into the child's thoughts, causing the relationship to deteriorate or become nonexistent.

Many people who have children are just not meant to be parents. Children should understand this, but we must also teach them to respect and extend grace to the absent parent.

If you could change one thing about your experience as the "new" parent or being raised by one, what would it be and why?

I would have held my mother more accountable. She didn't raise me, but she raised other children. Unfortunately, due to her addiction, her inability or refusal to show up for her children was simply excused, as my grandmother (her mother) never held her accountable. As a result, she never stepped up.

How can society better support parents and their families?

Society can better support by building and encouraging villages to help raise children. It truly does take a village to raise a child. We need more encouragement and resources, especially for those who are elderly and raising children. Older adults are often on fixed incomes and may not be proficient in technology, so there must be a village of all ages to assist.

Please share a memorable story or anecdote from your experience related to this scenario.

Many people wanted to celebrate with me when I graduated from college in 2015. As a first-generation college graduate, relatives wanted to ride down to Atlanta from DC to attend, but it was still unclear if my mother would be there. My grandparents drove down at the last minute due to my mother's indecisiveness, and she ultimately did not come. Though it could have been an upsetting moment for me, as many family members were extremely disappointed, I felt relieved and appreciative of those who attended. Honestly, I had already released all expectations and hurt that stemmed from her history of never showing up for me. That day, I learned that we cannot place expectations on people who expect nothing from themselves.

What is the most valuable lesson you learned from your experience?

My most valuable lesson is always to express gratitude for life and know that circumstances cannot alter or deter me from greatness. Certain experiences shape us into who we are, how we think, and even how we move around in this world; however, it should never make us feel guilty or hindered from all that we desire to experience in life. No matter how we start, life can be great, and we can excel.

Is there anything else you would like to add or share that would be important for others to know about this life?

There should be more conversation on the effects of parental abandonment and neglect and the impact of being raised by someone other than a biological parent.

Ashley's Story

Describe the circumstances that led you to be raised by someone other than your parents.

My mother died when I was five years old, so my grandmother raised me. When my mother passed away, she was 25 years old. She was diagnosed with juvenile diabetes at the age of nine. She had diabetes, but it was kidney failure that really took a toll on her. Yet, everyone who knew her called her Bobcat because she was said to have nine lives. She would always reappear like nothing happened after being declared dead.

She'd had a miscarriage before I was born, and the doctors advised her to avoid pregnancy. My father would say I was a surprise. Despite the doctors' advice to end the pregnancy, Mom insisted that I was the girl she had prayed for. Even before the doctor told her my gender, she already knew. Although she was warned that having a child would shorten her life, she wanted her daughter, and then I came along.

How did you first learn about your unique family dynamics, and what were your initial thoughts and feelings?

My mother prepared me for her death long before she passed away. She would frequently impart new knowledge to me, warning, "I need you to know this because I will not always be here with you."

What were some challenges you faced?

With what she had, my grandmother did the best she could. She was much older than other parents, and I often got the impression that because of her age, we would avoid discussing sex, boys, love, and real-life experiences. Despite my highly insulated upbringing, I learned from my friends' decisions.

How did your relationship with your new family shape your childhood and adolescence?

I often claim to have had the best of both worlds because I was close to both sides of my family. It was unusual because, although my maternal grandmother did not play, my grandma on my dad's side was not as strict. My family is tight on both sides to this day. I gained a lot of knowledge.

In what ways do you feel your upbringing was different from your peers?

Being raised by a strict grandmother made me terrified of a lot of things, and I was prohibited from dating. I was constantly the object of curiosity for guys, but my grandmother would have none of it. I assume my grandmother wanted me to avoid the difficulties of teenage pregnancy since she'd had her first child at the age of 17.

What positive aspects or strengths did you gain from being raised in this situation?

I grew up exceptionally different from my peers because my grandmother was in her late 80s. Being raised by my grandmother gave me access to a wealth of knowledge that most of my peers seldom received from their parents. Laughably, my judgmental personality was much ahead of its time, but I had picked it up from an elder who refused to hold back her opinion. My grandmother taught me many life lessons; figuratively speaking, I could always see things coming from a mile away.

What advice would you give someone who has found themselves in this situation?

Show empathy and care for others. People did not believe how aware I was of my circumstances because I was young, but I knew. My mother had imparted a great deal of information about how life would be altered once she departed and numerous warnings.

What support systems or resources were most helpful to you in your experience?

I had no resources at all. My large family was entirely dependent upon one another. Seeing a psychiatrist was unheard of in the 1990s. And let's face it: if you told someone you planned to get professional help back then, they would probably assume you were crazy.

What strategies did you find effective in managing this situation's emotional and practical challenges?

It's a process you never fully get over; all you can do is learn how to cope and move on. I've noticed that I'm more sensitive about not having a mother as an adult than I was when I was younger.

What is the most important thing for parents to remember as they navigate this unexpected journey?

Above all else, I advise that they be understanding. It can sometimes be challenging to comprehend the new standard, let alone accept it. Although I was aware that my mother had passed away, there were still a lot of unanswered questions.

If you could change one thing about your experience as the "new" parent or being raised by one, what would it be and why?

I believe I would have advanced in life by now if I had more freedom to pursue my interests. I had to learn everything as an adult due to my grandmother's desire to shield me. She didn't know that by avoiding certain subjects, she was doing more harm than good.

How can society better support parents and their families?

Never hesitate to seek the assistance of a competent expert or counselor to guide you through the phases of grief. My grandmother continues to say that she wishes she could have gotten us the professional help we both needed but never received. We had a deep connection because her mother had also passed away when she was just two weeks old.

What is the most valuable lesson you learned from your experience?

A book should never be judged by its cover. People would pity me as a child, and I was not too fond of it. I was never depressed or needy. My life wasn't horrible. The only difference between me and other kids was that my mom was dead. Besides that and my grandmother's strict guidelines, my life was "pretty lit," as the kids say.

Is there anything else you would like to add or share that would be important for others to know about this life?

When it comes to death, people frequently seek to assign blame. Death is inevitable. You must die one day to be born. That's just the way things are. No one is to blame for it. Enjoy life while it lasts since everyone has an expiration date, and we can never be sure of the exact moment it will end.

Janice's Story

Describe the circumstances that led you to be raised by someone other than your parents.

At the age of 5, my stepfather went to prison, and due to my mother's lifestyle, she thought it would be safe if my little brother and I lived with my grandparents. At the time, she was a big-time drug dealer and involved in a gang. Though they were both heavily involved in the lifestyle before my stepfather's incarceration, she believed that she couldn't raise us alone and felt her only choice was to send us to our grandparents' house.

How did you first learn about your unique family dynamics, and what were your initial thoughts and feelings?

Although I was very young, I knew my life had drastically changed. Actually, it worsened because my stepfather had played a significant role in my life before going to prison. When my living situation changed, it affected me at school, and I started to fail in 2nd grade. My grandparents were amazing people, but I wanted my parents. Not to mention, my biological father was in and out of the picture. I was sad; I felt abandoned, and nothing seemed to matter to anyone.

What were some challenges you faced?

Since my grandmother was raising me, my hairstyles and clothing were that of an older person, which incited the kids at school to tease me. When there were campus events or parent meetings, my grandmother showed up, not my mom.

At five years old, I still lived at home and had my own room with all my toys. There wasn't space for them after moving into my grandparents' house; I had to share a room with my brother and step-uncle. I was forced to leave it all behind.

How did your relationship with your new family shape your childhood and adolescence?

My relationship with my grandparents was great. They did the best they could.

As a child, I remember us sitting at the dinner table together, which created a bond. And on holidays, we engaged in fun family activities. My grandmother taught me many things that I will forever be grateful for. They showed me so much love and protected me.

I also learned structure within a household and how to carry myself, which stuck with me even after being allowed to return to my mom. My grandmother was very strict in certain areas and taught me etiquette. I was sheltered in many ways, which caused me to be guarded, but I look forward to breaking away from being closed in when I have the chance.

In what ways do you feel your upbringing was different from your peers?

When raised by older people, there will be some missed opportunities and activities. Many friends went to amusement parks, had parties, and lived freely. Contrarily, my grandmother had rules and was very strict, so I was told to stay in the house and be off the phone by a specific time.

What positive aspects or strengths did you gain from being raised in this situation?

This situation taught me how to maintain my household. I am well-mannered, and as a woman, I carry myself well. The negative things that happened in my mother's home and prevented me from living with her make me ensure that my own children are not exposed to those types of environments. The adversity also caused me to have a strong and healthy relationship with my children.

What advice would you give someone who has found themselves in this situation?

Life can and will be hard. Take every lesson, good and bad, and use it as a tool to build a brighter future.

What support systems or resources were most helpful to you in your experience?

I found that having a community is great. Get around like-minded individuals. Seek therapy if you need it, and make healing from past trauma a priority.

What strategies did you find effective in managing this situation's emotional and practical challenges?

I prioritize self-care, and my commitment to therapy and doing the work has helped me tremendously. Identifying the root cause of my issues, whether it's rejection, abandonment, etc., has been crucial to my healing.

What is the most important thing for parents to remember as they navigate this unexpected journey?

If you must put your children in unexpected situations due to life events, remember that they are human beings with feelings and a voice. Take the time to know how they feel and allow them to express themselves fully.

If you could change one thing about your experience as the "new" parent or being raised by one, what would it be and why?

My only wish is that I had the opportunity to be heard. I was placed with my grandparents for my safety, which I understand, but the inability to express how I felt greatly affected me.

How can society better support parents and their families?

I believe having more resources, holding more conversations on various family dynamics and experiences, and creating resolutions for these families will better support parents and their families.

Please share a memorable story or anecdote from your experience related to this scenario.

As a child living with my mom, my room was decorated nicely. I had the Mickey Mouse phone, the fake kitchen set with all the groceries to go with it, and the washer and dryer. For a 5-year-old, my room was really hooked up. I reflect on it now and realize it was a vision being created of the life I wanted—one of a well-put-together home. I felt robbed of it at some point when I had to move into my grandparents' house.

As I dwell in my current home, which I built for myself, I recognize that while being displaced as a child may have been painful, it was a part of my story. It took that experience to build everything I have now, even though it felt like I was being torn down.

What is the most valuable lesson you learned from your experience?

To any individual with a rough past, who has trauma, or who experiences loneliness and failure, don't be discouraged. Your start does not determine your end. Use your life experiences to build a greater future.

Samantha's Story

Describe the circumstances that led you to be raised by someone other than your parents.

My daughter was a meth addict. She came to my house on her birthday with a black eye and asked for $20. I insisted that she go to rehab, and she agreed. Since her three children were at her sister's house, my husband and I went to pick them up, and they never went home to her after that. Since then, we have adopted the three children in addition to their baby sister, who was meth-addicted at birth.

What were your initial feelings and reactions when you took on this role?

I thought she would get them back. I didn't fully know what meth addicts were capable of—giving up everything for the high. I gave her two months before I called DHS on her.

How did your priorities and daily routines change after becoming a new parent?

I had to change jobs. I was working from home for a towing company as a dispatcher, but I couldn't answer phones with children screaming or asking tons of questions in the background. I went back to college, got a degree, and changed careers.

What were your biggest challenges, and how did you overcome them?

Money. We were comfortable when it was just the two of us, but adding three mouths was difficult.

How did this experience affect your relationships with friends, family, and community?

Our adult children were very jealous of how we raised them because it wasn't how they were raised. They would question why we didn't discipline them the same. We were definitely more demanding of our own children.

In what ways has this situation changed you as a person?

I've become bitter. I used to be an outgoing, happy-go-lucky person. Now, all I can think about are the kids and how unfair it is that I am raising them and not able to enjoy my own life.

What advice would you give someone who has found themselves in a similar situation?

As hard as it is, be strong for the kids; they didn't ask for this, and they don't really know what's happening. Be prepared for numerous questions when they are older, and be truthful, but keep answers at their maturity level.

What support systems or resources were most helpful to you?

Mental health professionals. Get as much help as you can from them.

What strategies did you find effective in managing emotional and practical challenges?

Strategies? I live day by day. If something worked yesterday, it may not work today. I go with the flow.

What is the most important thing for parents to remember as they navigate this unexpected journey?

Your daughter or son is still there; don't beat yourself up over their adult decisions. You did your absolute best with what knowledge you had while raising them. Their actions do not define you as a parent.

How can society better support parents and their families?

Don't forget that we are human too. Ask us out for coffee, or ask if we need to talk. Don't abandon the grandparents who stepped up when no one else could or would.

Please share a memorable story or anecdote from your experience related to this scenario.

Most memorable is the feeling I get when I advocate for one of the children and something finally comes to fruition. My grandson is eight now, but we've had him since he was 16 months old. I've always believed he had Autism, and he's had several issues with being a "normal" kid. He was often in his own world. I demanded accommodations for him at school that others found ridiculous for a 3-year-old in preschool. In pre-kindergarten, I requested an IEP and received one without him attending school for the recommended length of time.

For years, I advocated for him to be tested, and twice he was—once at six and again at seven. The final testing came when we had no choice but to place him in a mental health facility for killing our dog and hurting his little sister. Finally, we found a doctor who understood our plight and could properly diagnose him with Autism. He is still in placement but at home as often as possible.

The advocacy doesn't stop there. Now, I am working toward getting my grandson into an Autism-focused facility that can help him. His current placement can't care for him in a way that enables him to function well in life and manage his emotions and behaviors.

What is the most valuable lesson you learned from your experience?

To not give up.

Is there anything else you would like to add or share that you think would be important for others to know?

It takes a mentally strong person to care for others. Don't let anyone tell you that you are doing something wrong or correct how you do it. No, it's not a fair life, but the chosen life makes a difference.

CHAPTER SEVEN

Dear Diary

As you navigate this journey of raising a child due to trauma, incarceration, or addiction, it's crucial to recognize and celebrate the strength, resilience, and love that fuel your path. The following diary pages should be used as a dedicated space for reflection, expression, and connection. They serve as a personal sanctuary where you can explore your thoughts, feelings, and experiences in writing. Use these pages to write love letters to yourself, your child, and your support system, utilizing Chapter Two's transformative "Joy Balm" technique.

The "Joy Balm" technique is a powerful tool designed to nurture your emotional well-being through positive and loving self-expression. Just as a balm soothes and heals the skin, the words you write can soothe and heal your soul. This practice involves writing love letters that celebrate your journey, acknowledge your efforts, and foster a deep sense of self-compassion and gratitude. By incorporating the "Joy Balm" technique into your diary entries, you can cultivate a mindset of positivity and resilience.

ABOUT THE AUTHOR

Adrienne Alexander is an author and the owner of the IPY Agency, a leading public relations firm representing entrepreneurs and individuals in the entertainment, lifestyle, and wellness spaces. As a former journalist, Adrienne has honed her storytelling and communication skills, which she now channels into her writing. She is celebrated for her children's books, which tackle delicate topics that often go unspoken. Adrienne's books are known for their sensitivity and insight, providing young readers and their families with a thoughtful exploration of important issues. Her dedication to crafting meaningful narratives that resonate with readers of all ages sets her apart as a unique and impactful voice in children's literature. She has also authored books on conflict resolution public relations and has released two journals.

www.ingramcontent.com/pod-product-compliance
Lightning Source LLC
Chambersburg PA
CBHW020322030826
48979CB00022B/759

* 9 7 9 8 9 8 8 4 6 2 0 1 9 *